Worlds Of Fantasy

Edited By Lisa Lowrie

CH00727154

First published in Great Britain in 2017 by:

Young Writers
Remus House
Coltsfoot Drive
Peterborough
PE2 9BF
Telephone: 01733 890066
Website: www.youngwriters.co.uk

All Rights Reserved
Book Design by Spencer Hart
© Copyright Contributors 2017
SB ISBN 978-1-78820-118-6
Printed and bound in the UK by BookPrintingUK
Website: www.bookprintinguk.com
YB0326EZ

FOREWORD

Young Writers is proud to present, 'Welcome To Wonderland –
Worlds Of Fantasy'.

For our latest competition, we invited secondary school pupils to
write a hundred word story set in a fantasy land or alternative
world of their own creation. This could be a positive magical place
where dreams come true or a dark, war-torn climate.

Dystopian fiction is hugely popular with young adult readers and
this competition gave aspiring writers the chance to create their
own vision of what the future could be like, from totalitarian
politics to post-apocalyptic landscapes. The results are
imaginative, insightful and often frightening.

Although a difficult task to bring a whole new world to life in such
few words, pupils rose to the challenge in creating their
Wonderlands, making use of descriptive language and building
atmosphere. The resulting collection is diverse and fascinating,
containing everything from natural disasters to futuristic lands
where technology has taken over.

I would like to congratulate all the authors featured in this
anthology and I hope it encourages you to keep writing!

Lisa Lowrie

CONTENTS

Izzy Hardy (14)	67
Sophie Knight (12)	68
Megan Drew (12)	69
Ellie-Mae Harfield (12)	70
Aimee Rous (12)	71
Summer Jones (12)	72
Lily-Mae Cross (12)	73
Sinead O'Neill (13)	74
Harriet Cahill (13)	75

The Vale Academy, Brigg

Amelia Summerton (13)	76
Amy Taylor (12)	77
Thomas Hewis	78
Shannon Pearson (11)	79
Adam Skinn	80
Aisling Skye Ellis (12)	81
Poppy May Merrifield (13)	82
Charlie Robinson (12)	83
Georgia Tock (11)	84
Jake Houghton (11)	85
Hannah Shearwood (12)	86
Charlotte Clark (13)	87
Alex Atkinson (12)	88
Thomas Armstrong (13)	89
Ross Smith (13)	90
Euan Hall (12)	91
Tom Nightingale (11)	92
James Goude (11)	93
Abbie Lammiman (12)	94
Archie Williamson (12)	95
Freya Watson (12)	96
Oliver Whitaker (12)	97
Selena May Capp (11)	98
Jake Forman (12)	99
Casey Griffin (12)	100
Faith Elizabeth Cavill (12)	101
Katie Johnson (12)	102

Ysgol Gyfun Llangefni, Llangefni

Cerys Vernon (13)	103
Mia Pritchard Evans (14)	104

Ysgol Y Preseli, Crymych

Ella Wintle (12)	105
Olivia Dobney (11)	106
Brooke Amy Evans-Harries (12)	107
Angharad Jones (12)	108
Will Parrott (12)	109
Iolo Griffiths (12)	110
Steffan Thomas (12)	111
Freya Watkins-Williams (11)	112
Nell Evans (11)	113
Evan Watts (12)	114
Mair Wilshaw (12)	115
Thomas William Nicholas (11)	116
Freddy Larsen (11)	117
Ffion Ann Peregrine (12)	118
Catrin Bishop (12)	119
Erin Rees-James (12)	120
Manon John (11)	121
Jemma Pinkney (12)	122
Hetty Lort-Phillips (12)	123
Ifan Thomas (12)	124
Sophie Louise Philipsen (14)	125
Seren Lewis (11)	126
Ruby Emma Travis (11)	127
Seren Rees (11)	128
Efa Gardner (11)	129
Ruben Mansfield (13)	130
Katey-Anne Othen (12)	131
Ben Blewitt (11)	132
Rhys Ouseley (12)	133
Ella Picton-Thomas (13)	134
Charlotte Caitlin Pickford (13)	135
John Griffith (12)	136
Niamh Grant (14)	137
Lowri Pritchard (12)	138
Maya Oyibo-Goss (14)	139
Ash Robarts	140
Hafwen Jenkins (12)	141

THE MINI SAGAS

From Sun City To... Sun City

'Paulo,' shouted Roberto, 'open the portal.' Paulo did as he was asked and using his own contraption, opened a portal from Sun City to somewhere they could only assume was far, far away. Roberto jumped into the portal and exited on the other side. However, still being surrounded by the tall glass buildings of Sun City he got confused. 'Paulo! It didn't work.'

At this moment a short, thin, tanned man came along and asked, 'What didn't work?'

Roberto turned around, 'Who are you?' he remarked.

'I am Leonardo. Where did you come from?'

'I don't know now,' replied Roberto.

Adam Hemmings (14)

Sandy Upper School, Sandy

London Has Fallen

'Heil Hitler!' thousands shouted in unison, as the man himself stood on the balcony of Buckingham Palace. Devastatingly, his words struck fear into the hearts of most. The realisation that this man was now the country's leader, ruler, controller... control. Full and undeniable power. Everywhere, red flags bearing the Swastika were waved high in the air, creating an awesome and intimidating atmosphere. 'Is this really life from now on, is this really our reality?' whispered Harry, heart breaking.
'I don't know,' replied Reggie, 'but it will take a lot of wrongs, before we can finally make things right.'

Ross Cahill (15)
Sandy Upper School, Sandy

Darkness

A small metal bunker stood on the precipice of a colossal mountain. From the metal structure was an amazing view of the picturesque valley coated in trees that were prised apart to form a river. Two men hiked up the mountain towards the silver tin. 'What's the time?' Bob asked, with a tone of unease.

'Don't worry, it's half five, we have an hour before it gets dark,' Jim replied.

Thirty minutes later, Bob and Jim were still on the ascent to their bunker, however, so was the darkness. Suddenly, the silence was shattered by blood-curdling shrieks. 'They're early!'

'R-r-run!'

Declan Welch (14)

Sandy Upper School, Sandy

Victoria's Last Appointment

I slashed straight through her silk-layered dress to her protruding abdomen, blood erupted, painting the surgery ruby red. Her pallid skin indicated her life trickling away. My gloved hand plunged into her, ripping her uterus out.
I twiddled the rubbery organ between my fingers, admiring the masterpiece.
I carefully placed the delicate organ on the desk beside my final letter, signed with my nickname given by the media. Jack the Ripper. I left the private surgery abandoning my lifeless, powerless royal patient behind. My job is done. My identity is revealed. I, Sir William Gull, am Jack the Ripper.

Robyn Lunt (15)
Sandy Upper School, Sandy

JFK's America

A dull metallic car ambled down the empty street, past lifeless houses. It was curfew so no one was allowed outside. Jay shot a jaded look over the paper-laden table to Alex and Jasmine. 'Are we really going to do this?' he sighed.

Jasmine muttered, 'I'm ready when you two are.'

Slowly, Alex gestured towards the circled map. 'It'll be difficult, and it might not even work,' Alex confessed dutifully. 'If it goes wrong we will die - no argument there. But to ensure the future of the world, we need to do it.'

'OK,' Jay said, 'let's kill JKF.'

Jordan James Irvin (15)
Sandy Upper School, Sandy

Doppelgänger

'This must be him!' Shep growled. Slowly stumbling over his feet, I had to keep him from exploding. He'd finally come face-to-face with his doppelgänger, but it was different. That thing framed Shepard for dozens of murders... it's time to get revenge. I removed my shaky hands from his forceful arm as he pulled away. Only recently we had both discovered how to stop the disguised creature, so our fear was replaced with hate. Both Shep and I, with erupting anger, sprang into the doppelgänger who was metres behind. The wooden stake then pierced him. It was over...

Kayleigh Boado
Sandy Upper School, Sandy

Dystopia

It had been two years since the fighting had started... the world turned to ash. Many people have perished, the rest left to live in hell. People once called this Earth. Now everyone calls this Dystopia. Living hell! Barry and Phil were two of the survivors. Unbelievable fear struck them.
Two years ago, when anarchy took over and all order dropped, the world went crazy. Now they live in abandoned New York, which is what they had to do to survive. 'What was that?' stuttered Barry.
'Go check!' shouted Phil. Constantly having to look over their shoulder, in this hell!

Oliver Hamilton (15)

Sandy Upper School, Sandy

Bitten

Gazing down in horror, her pulsing artery flowed down like a waterfall. An unimaginable hunger flowed through her veins. Confused, alone and distressed, Isabel exclaimed, 'Help!' No one was around to help her. Nearly giving up hope, Isabel searched around her for answers. Picturesque scenery was wrapped around her. The sounds of a waterfall sounded deafening to her ear. Dazed in a frenzy of panic, Isabel noticed her neck had completely healed. A dark shadow approached her and whispered, 'I know what you are, I can help you. Come with me to Everlasting.' Isabel ran.

Emily Garlick (15)
Sandy Upper School, Sandy

The Fall

'Quick Sam, it's time to go.' I was reluctant but, at Jack's call, I pulled the Brazilian with me. Staring at the dystopia we caused was disheartening. I guess that's what you get when three cybernetic soldiers attempt to free civilisation from corrupt governments making everything perfect. We were all blind. Our city 13, in ruins. 'At least the people were free,' muttered Sam. His long hair blew in the gentle breeze, coasting over our position on the wall. But we no longer belong here. The end for us now comes. Now it's finally our time. Our time to fall.

Carrie Martin (14)
Sandy Upper School, Sandy

The Running Dead

'Get him!' Alan shouts as the crooked criminal is crashed off
the road. 'Down on your knees!' Alan commanded as the
criminal reluctantly stepped out from his vehicle. All of a
sudden, the wonky-eyed criminal whipped a gun from
behind himself and shot Alan in the leg!
Fourteen years later, Alan woke from his coma through
bleary eyes, and the room in perfect condition. Get
well cards lay next to him. However, as the bearded man
walked out the room, it was a completely different story.
Zombies stumbling around in the corridor soon alerted the
thirty-six year-old man!

Josh Dooley (15)
Sandy Upper School, Sandy

Jumping Through Space

Flash! Tumbling through a darker than black void (courtesy of the crystal I touched), I shiver with fear as I anticipate what will come. Suddenly, a world materialises before me, a vast stretch of golden sand appears in heatwaves. I attempt to move but my legs are immobile. Why does it appear I'm moving? Flickering metres away, I glimpse at another glowing crystal, I must make a leap for it. *Whoosh*, an enormous snowball bulldozes the stationary me like a wrecking ball. Seconds later, as I reach for the crystal again, a tsunami tries to wash me away. *Flash!*

Holly Szasz (15)
Sandy Upper School, Sandy

Knowledgeless

In 5073 Earth has advanced dramatically, robots rule the streets. In 5009 the current ruler decided to dismiss education and implant knowledge chips into people's brains once they'd reached eighteen. I woke up to a bright, white light and what must be a dozen medic bots encompassing me. The operation was over, aside from my aching head, I didn't seem to feel anything. Slowly, others woke up from their knowledge and revelation. I couldn't help but feel jealous; why hadn't the chip worked? Worries clouded in my head like mist. The operation had not worked.

Petra Ruby May Easton (15)
Sandy Upper School, Sandy

Split Worlds

'Fine!' Rio stormed up the stairs and slammed his bedroom door ferociously. The booming bang shook the surrounding walls. After pounding the pillows on his bed, he clenched his fists and forced his eyes to close. Anger pierced through his body making him shake. Until... shockingly, he felt a cool breeze sway through his ruffled hair. It was clear, he wasn't in his bedroom any more. Slowly, he allowed his eyes to open. The heaving in his chest stopped abruptly and was replaced by a gasp. Where was he? He was not certain, but he was sure it was Utopia!

Caitlin Thomas (14)
Sandy Upper School, Sandy

Battle Of The Clans

'Aah!' screamed the female clan as they ran towards the male clan with weapons. Screaming, shouting and crying coming from all directions as war broke out between the two genders. Who will win? No one knows. Zyana, leader of the females, was pushing her team forward to victory, while Rada, the leader of the males, was trying his best not to declare defeat. Try as he might, Zyana's team was coming out stronger and more powerful. Thousands of females and males were dropping dead. As the battle started coming to an end, it was clear to see the winner. Females.

Aleesha Davies (15)
Sandy Upper School, Sandy

The Hidden Shadow

She was running that day, running through the golden meadow; pale, golden hair streaming behind her. Each year her family would go and break the one rule this world had. However, this time she went alone. I knew her family more than anyone else. People thought of them as the only criminals left. I knew otherwise. Emily's bravery was just stupidity. He was lurking there that day, knowing, waiting for her. He was my secret, hidden from the world. I controlled him and his only setting was brutality. Emily? She was never to be seen again; to my secret delight.

Kirsty Williams (14)
Sandy Upper School, Sandy

Shadows

He leant down to pick up the coin glinting in the sun, but as soon as his fingertips touched the cold metal, a bright light charged through his eyes. The path with smiling laughing children and a bright blue sky had changed to a grey world, with a pair of swings rocking in the eerily still sky. The faint sound of children laughing and the creak of old swings stopped. The silence swallowing him, seeing a shadow not belonging to himself, he spun around. Suddenly, fingers wrapped around his shoulder, forcing him into the ground; now there were two shadows.

Freya Nicholson-Clinch (15)
Sandy Upper School, Sandy

12/12/12

It was 12/12/12 at 12.11pm. Everybody was frightened, distressed and petrified. You could smell the intense fear all around. We all stuck together like glue. My family and my three cats. Waiting for the clock to strike 12.12 was taking forever. I was trembling with fear. Tears like liquid silver slipped down my face with my heart beating furiously fast, I felt it would escape. It was ten seconds from now. I couldn't believe it. I'd only lived ten years of my life. Swiftly, it became three seconds. We all counted down out loud together. '3... 2... 1.'

Jakia Jasmin Nessa (15)
Sandy Upper School, Sandy

The Woodland

The woodland was once the only safe place. A traumatising war corrupted our land, leaving corpses to drown in their own blood. It was a Tuesday afternoon when I skidded underneath the barb wired fence. The monster-like trees glaring down at me with their twisted branches, looking like fingers and hissing like a snake. I slowly strolled through, making sure I wasn't caught as I approached a shelter made from twigs and leaves. But just at that moment, I heard a horrifying shriek and a shadow approaching me, slowly backing up, my leg caught a log. This was it...

Melissa Gay (15)

Sandy Upper School, Sandy

Ants' Hostility

It started out as a normal day, sunny. Happy. It was great...
then the ground exploded... out they climbed, huge jaws
built to kill. Nothing could stop their rampage. Buildings
crumbled, trees toppled and all the children screamed. They
must have had a huge nest underground as they appeared
from all directions at once.

Days later, I met my first survivor. I called out to him. He
paused. Turned and waved. I tried to warn him but it
happened so fast... He was dead. From then on I was wary.
And you should be too. Beware... it's hostile out there.

Nathan Endersby (14)
Sandy Upper School, Sandy

The Abandoned Earth

The city was almost silent; aside from the voices that followed me constantly. With a gun in my hand (protection from the remaining rabid dogs that pounced when disturbed) I crept down the street towards my shack. I froze when I felt warm breath tickle my neck, making me shiver, and to my horror, I spotted a large black shadow behind me. Quickly, I spun around; nothing. I cautiously turned to continue, then I saw her. A girl with sunken black eyes, wearing a shabby nightgown, staring at me. Raising her bony finger to point at me, she stomped closer...

Rhianna Nicole Walsingham (15)
Sandy Upper School, Sandy

Survivor's Guilt

The knife rattles like glass panes in a window frame during a violent earthquake, in my equally unstable hands, with the blade pointing towards a dusty, fragile, ginger cat. Who am I kidding? I can't kill that. But if I don't eat, there'll soon be nothing left of me. I squeeze the knife handle tighter as a distant screech of pure agony echoes through the desolate city. I freeze. Kill or be killed. Those words will forever linger in my mind. No matter how long this nightmare drags on, I will never get used to it. The thought terrifies me.

Rosie Yuji Elizabeth Gilks (15)

Sandy Upper School, Sandy

Old Man Jenkins

She tried escaping the wrath of Old Man Jenkins, she knew going into his ghost house was not right, however, she needed to know. She had to know... what happened to her dad in this house? Many people warned her that Old Man Jenkins lived in this ghostly house. She ran down the corridor and Old Man Jenkins was soon on her tail. She dashed up the stairs where Old Man Jenkins followed. She soon lost Jenkins and, without thinking, hid in the closet. After a while, Old Man Jenkins ripped her out! Screaming, she noticed Jenkins was her dad...

Rio Joseph Samuels (15)

Sandy Upper School, Sandy

The New Planet

A family of five discovered a new planet and wanted to go there, so they did and it was covered in jungle-like plants and deadly animals, so deadly that they killed the little baby girl. The family was devastated but they carried on their investigation of their new planet. They kept walking and walking until they came across a volcano which they decided to stay near but that night there was a rumble, the volcano was erupting and the whole planet was dying because there was no water and was even covered in lava. The people very sadly died.

Charlotte Porter
Sandy Upper School, Sandy

The World Beneath

It wasn't always like this. They didn't always have to hide.
Shape-shifters and humans, they got along. The world
beneath now live in peace and the world of humans in
prejudice. Evangeline and Evan were young and unwise,
they set out across their haven to the ever hidden world of
the humans. As the siblings emerged into the chaos, they
looked around in awe. This was not expected. A heavily
armoured human swung round and pointed a gun at them
before shouting, 'Shape-shifter! Mongrels!' and they ducked
and escaped them.

Ellis Blake (15)
Sandy Upper School, Sandy

The Forbidden Princess

I didn't know how I'd gotten into this situation. One second I'd been running and the next I was stuck in a cold, dark room. I'd been stripped of all my family heirlooms and my crown for a crime I didn't commit. Why would I kill all of the villagers? It didn't make sense. I knew my fate. I knew I'd be executed, my robes given to my miserable mother for her to burn. I wasn't scared. If anything, I was ready for it. It was the waiting that hurt. 'Annabella! Time is up!' My time was over at last.

Faith Warren (15)

Sandy Upper School, Sandy

The Great Battle

One day, everyone who lived on Rainbow Wonderland came together and had a huge party. There were different people on the world. As we were setting the party up, there was a knock at the gates and a man walked in. He looked straight at me and smirked. Then the gates were broken and a huge army came in. It was the Ughs, they were always unhappy. We fought for four hours straight. I had to protect us. So I led the armies into battle. We killed their leader and lived happily ever after. We celebrated with the huge party.

Charlotte Morgan (14)
Sandy Upper School, Sandy

The Fall Of Roborthia

The planet of Roborthia was a very calm and peaceful place, with all the humans living together in harmony and the robots all built for doing all the work for humans, so that they could all spend time together. One person didn't like this idea and wanted to kill the robot king, so robots and humans were equal. He has already failed two assassination attempts, but his third one had to work! As he was about to assassinate the king, the king saw him and convinced him not to, because it would destroy the civilisation they lived in.

Ethan David Stout (14)
Sandy Upper School, Sandy

Evil Becomes Good!

A girl called Elena lived in a magical world called Mysteryland. She was an ordinary young girl who had a happy life, until one day a nasty, horrible woman took over their world. Elena got fed up of the evil queen, so she decided to do something about it. Friends and family didn't believe she could do it.

The next day, she walked through the woods to the big castle. She dressed as a guard so she could blend in. Elena didn't know she had powers. Elena beat the queen with her powers and every person was happy now.

Erin Simms

Sandy Upper School, Sandy

Tryland Mystery

A boy called Tommy lived in the world of Tryland with his family. One day his family went out for a walk around Tryland. Tommy didn't think Tryland was amazing like other places. There were no big cities, big buildings or nice beaches. It was just many villages surrounded by trees. He thought this until he got lost on the walk. He didn't know what to do on his own. He saw strange animals he had never seen before. He met new people, found new places. He was very disappointed when he had to go back home to normal life.

Kristen Pask (13)
Sandy Upper School, Sandy

I Am Joe Bryan

I'm Joe Bryan. I have seen the world being torn apart in front of me, by vicious creatures. Every night I lay, listening to them, screeching, clawing, desperate to get at me. They used to be human. Before the outbreak. As I condensate the stone cold pane of glass with my rapid breaths, the foregrip of my M16 held tightly in my clammy hand. My eyes narrow as my free hand slowly and silently lifts up the window frame. I take my aim, and pull the trigger for the final time, except not at the zombies. At my own head.

Jamie McEvoy (14)
Sandy Upper School, Sandy

The Magic House

Chloe's eyes lit up as she saw a new shiny doll's house in the middle of her small room. She dashed straight towards the house and picked up a doll. A flash of light lit up the room, as she dropped inside the house. The doll she had picked up was now standing beside her. They were both dressed in long dresses with gas masks round their necks. The doll led her outside where all the things she never believed in were there. Santa, unicorns and much more. But nothing was as it seemed! They were in World War Two.

Shannon Lewinton (14)
Sandy Upper School, Sandy

My Life As A Slave

I wake up every morning at 5.30 to shouting of guards and slaves, it's horrible. Once I am awake, I have to clean the bedrooms and toilets, it's disgusting. Once we have done that, it's time for breakfast. Gruel today. We have five minutes to eat it. Next we have to go to the deck and we get tied up so we can't go anywhere. We have to clean, clean, clean. Once we've finished, it's about 6.00. We have ten minutes to eat dinner. Cold soup. Then we have to go to bed. The next day will be even worse.

Kristina Peat (13)

Sandy Upper School, Sandy

A New Beginning

As I woke up from my chamber I noticed I was the only one left in the vault. As my body defrosted I fell and slammed into the cold, wet floor. I slowly stumbled to my feet and made my way towards the exit. As I got to the door I hit the big button and the vault door screeched open for the first time in 100 years. As the door opened I could see a barren wasteland covered in feral beasts and ghouls. As I looked over the barren wasteland, I realised this was a brand-new beginning.

Jacob Petrisor (14)
Sandy Upper School, Sandy

Harriet's Heaven

Harriet's deep blue eyes sparkled magnificently as she witnessed the glistening, golden gates open into a crisp, white view of pure cloud mountains. Her jaw dropped as five gigantic turquoise butterflies swooped past. Taking her first ambitious step into Heaven, she floated swiftly through the gates and a gleaming smile grew on her face as she realised what awaited her.

Surrounded by the unimaginable, Harriet danced to her mind's music and skipped joyfully through the soft, misty clouds while singing to songs of content.

With a heart of satisfaction, she leapt through the unthinkable land of her huge creative mind.

Libby Moors (13)
The Buckingham School, Buckingham

Welcome To Wonderland

'Welcome to Wonderland,' they said. 'It'll be fun,' they said. My first job. Working with little people, with the dragons and creatures. The rules were simple: don't feed the animals, don't run, but most of all, don't touch the animals. I didn't mean to...

I didn't want this to happen... They made me... The button wasn't touched... They escaped... They all chased me, I didn't know what was happening. Round this corner, round the bed, I'm running till the very end. I woke up... Gasping for breath... Covered in sweat... To find out, it was all just a horrible nightmare...

Sophie Cassidy (14)
The Buckingham School, Buckingham

The End

The tree radiated an illuminous golden light, enticing me towards it. There was a door, recklessly I twisted the handle, in front of me unfolded a view beyond belief. Miniature wooden houses stretched across the horizon. It dawned on me they belong to the thousands of squirrels, who were glaring at me. The creatures who seemed harmless, caused fear to swell inside me as they turned nuts into potentially lethal projectiles. One, dressed in a general's military suit, spoke the words that would obliterate all humankind. 'Our foe has penetrated our territory, the war has now officially begun.'

Jessica Knight (13)
The Buckingham School, Buckingham

The Missing

I walk in through the front door sighing heavily. Chucking my bag on the kitchen table, I trudge upstairs. My mum calls out to me. 'Hey, you wanna move this bag of yours?'
'Yeah, in a minute,' I answer, rolling my eyes. Then I get an anonymous voicemail. 'How's your mum? Still missing?' Weird... but I just ignore it. Scrolling through Instagram something catches my eye. A missing poster and it's no ordinary poster. It's of my mum. But she's downstairs. Isn't she? Then the realisation sinks in. Where is she? And who is that woman walking up the stairs?

Lucy Atkins (13)
The Buckingham School, Buckingham

Alex In Slumberland

As Alex stumbled through the tiny wooden door, his rugged blonde locks soared through the air in a ginormous gust of wind. He looked upon to the pinkish-hued horizon with a blurred view. Mountains coasted the luscious heavens above. Eyes still adjusting to the magenta illumination. Orange shrubbery sprinkled over. Alex jogged into the sunset, awaiting for his dream-time adventure to begin. Racing through the blue coloured grass, he began to perceive an instant change in terrain. This was not hard rock though. This was the fur of a sleeping Flabber Wacky! Poor Alex had poked the beast.

Chris Lloyd (13)

The Buckingham School, Buckingham

The Mini-Brains!

'There is another sum in! Callum - come. It's a tricky one...'
A very long and complex sum popped up on the mini-brain
screen. They spent half an hour working it out, but in the
time of human, it was 3.5 seconds. 'Who's doing the night
shift?'
'I will!'
'Thanks!'
The atmosphere in the calculator was always so happy!
Everyone was friends. It sounds impossible but it shows us
how sick we are, as a race. Horrible people. This myth can
become reality if us humans have some love. Happiness.
The world would have peace!

Poppy Ann Clemency Fisher (12)
The Buckingham School, Buckingham

The Rabbit Hole

I fell down the rabbit hole; floating and sinking all at once. Stuck in-between with no end and no beginning, a hat and stopwatch. Further and further, was that a rabbit in a waistcoat? Falling, I'm still falling! A drunk caterpillar smoking among the dirt. Someone's dancing - a crazy man with fiery hair. He watches me. I'm still falling! No, not falling. I'm stuck - stuck in a never-ending fairy tale. A fairy tale with smartly dressed rabbits and a dancing mad man. There's blood. Blood on my hand, staining my dress. The knife agonisingly dragged out my heart.

Molly Mackay (14)
The Buckingham School, Buckingham

Welcome To Wonderland

Wonderland, a mystical place, filled with joy, fantasy and a place to encapsulate yourself with nothing but happiness. Until one day a young, beautiful girl galloping home was met by a foul monster. He had glistening sharp teeth that could puncture even stones, crimson-red eyes and a lust for blood, stronger than the will to live.

He lurked in the murky shadows apprehending his next target: the girl. Abruptly, she could feel his sharp, icy breath gliding across her fragile neck, searching for the perfect place to make the final kill. She turned around to meet her fate...

Abbi O'Flanagan (13)
The Buckingham School, Buckingham

Welcome To Wonderland

I was unprepared for what lay through the small, wooden door. I staggered through. My jaw inexplicably dropped in hesitation. A sudden warmth cursed through my veins as I caught glimpses of creatures I had no name for, dwarf-like animals which seemed to have a look of hilarity and madness etched on their disproportionate faces, even something that looked like candy canes, swaying in a dove-like way.

Something felt wrong, like it wasn't supposed to exist. Instinct was what drove me to capture a sight I could not quite hide from my mind. A sword raised, homing in...

Emily Cooper (13)
The Buckingham School, Buckingham

The Voice On The Stairs

There once was a boy who lived in a house with a grand staircase. One day, as the boy was walking towards the stairs, he heard, 'Play with me!' The boy did not answer but the voice said again, 'I bet you your life you can't come up these stairs!'

The boy ran up the stairs and the voice again said, 'I bet you you can't go down!'

The boy walked down and said, 'Goodbye now!'

Irritated, the voice said, 'I bet you your life you can't come up!'

'Yes,' he said. He ran up and never came down!

Genevieve Rose Commaille (12)

The Buckingham School, Buckingham

Winter Wonderland

'Welcome to Winter Wonderland,' said the king. Everywhere you go all you see is ice and snow and skaters. Everybody was great at their sport. Some people like Sascian Lizza and Philipa Horden had qualified for the Universal Figure Skating Championships as they had won the World Championships. They knew that if they came last their legacy would be ruined so they were determined to win. When they were at the competition, they knew they had trained their hardest and before they went on the ice they knew that if they skated the best possible they would always win.

Tamsin Baillie (11)
The Buckingham School, Buckingham

In The Dark

I turned a corner to find a dark corridor. My heart was thumping; lurking in the darkness I saw a pitch-black, cloak-wearing figure holding a rich-red, dripping bloodstained knife. It stared silently at me for a minute. I tried to be as quiet as a mouse. My heart stopped! The looming figure started pacing towards me. I turned round and, to my horror, it was standing right in front of me. I turned around again spinning, spinning, eyes facing me. I was surrounded by dark-cloaked figures. I closed my eyes; my hopes, my dreams, my life - all gone. Blackout...

Fleur Louise Collinge (12)
The Buckingham School, Buckingham

Welcome To Wonderland

As he awoke from his 100-year slumber, Lenk sat up in anticipation, yet he was confused as to what had happened, what had become of the world? Little did he know, it wasn't just the world that had changed, his mind had as well. He lost all recollection of what happened before he fell to slumber.

As he stared around the glowing, orange-veined cave, he heard a voice, a soft, recognisable voice... 'Lenk... Lenk... Save us, Lenk... Save us all.' Stepping out, he saw a world of drakes and goblins. He now knew why he was awoken again... Vengeance...

Ben Fowler (14)
The Buckingham School, Buckingham

Welcome To Wonderland

I stepped out from the smouldering wreckage and gawped in astonishment. Thousands of strange, alien, yet somehow beautiful creatures and plants surrounded me and glared at me, as if I'm a kitten on their doorstep. Dainty nymphs danced around my head and chimed the soft, near silent songs. I turned around to see dwarf-like creatures dismantling my plane. I screamed, running at them and shouting to leave it alone, when I felt a sharp prick on the back of my neck and the lights began to fade; in the back of my mind I quietly heard, 'Welcome to Wonderland!'

James Moss (14)
The Buckingham School, Buckingham

The Darkness

I see the curtains shivering, the window left open. It has left. When it enters, it brings havoc and pain. I sit down on the rickety floorboards, trying to calm myself, thinking back to the time I last saw it... I didn't dare meet it again. I remember; it staring at me, hovering over the dead dog it tortured then killed. It had torn open its stomach; guts, blood and various organs spilt across the floor. Looking up to its face, its jaw filled with blood, it gave me a menacing look and dissolved through the open window. It'll return!

Nikita Kalsi (13)

The Buckingham School, Buckingham

The Dragon War

There was fire, darkness and anger in their eyes... *Flash!* Suddenly, hundreds of enormous figures merged out of the sky. It turned as dark as the night sky, then a sudden ear-splitting sound came. Their wings were as long as a plane, their claws were as sharp as daggers and their squawk was deafening to hear. Within seconds, the small, innocent town was in flames. The fire was red and reeked like smoke. They came for revenge, revenge, revenge. From that day the world became dark and grey. The frightening fire and misty smoke took many lives. Rest in peace.

April Barnes (13)
The Buckingham School, Buckingham

Welcome To Wonderland

Suddenly, Jack's being chased by a mythical beast who possesses a chainsaw. He runs until he is cornered. Nowhere to go. Nowhere but the afterlife. However, just as the beast goes to strike, it appears. A door. A creaky, dark door that slowly opens. It's his only hope.

Jack ventures on, to be confronted by a deep hole. He jumped, but never landed. Would he ever land? All of a sudden his question is answered. *Bang!* Rough, ridged concrete touches his face. His life is over. But he is fine, untouched. He looks up to see the magical wonderland...

James Peat (14)
The Buckingham School, Buckingham

Walking In Wonderland

I am Emily, an explorer stuck in Wonderland. I take my chance to look around at the wonderful, mystical sights this deserted place has to offer. As far as I know I am the first person to set foot in this magical valley in the middle of the towering trees of the rainforest. Only animals for company. Beautiful and mind-blowing this place is, thousands of tiny meandering, sapphire-painted rivers glistening in the light of the huge flaming sun beating down. Big, green bushes surround this mesmerising place with sweet-smelling colourful berries. Do I really want to leave?

Sophie Coombes (11)
The Buckingham School, Buckingham

Welcome To Wonderland

Bright vibrant colours surrounded me. The sky was painted colours of the rainbow, trees a baby pink, like candyfloss, the path in front was a stripy, multicoloured road. In awe of all the miraculous sights I was gazing at, I forgot to ask myself the question, where am I?

As I went to stand, a buzzing noise flew across my face. A creature that was unrealistic, that had never ever been seen before, or would. All these sights, all these smells, all these feelings. Whispers filled my ears, I slowly turned my head to the sights of something unbelievable...

Bethany Evans (14)

The Buckingham School, Buckingham

The Tree Of Treasures

When my family and I moved to the countryside from the city, I was in despair, a moody teen missing my friends. My Internet, my life. Being the impatient girl I am, I stormed out to explore the woods. I came across a tree, a rather magical appearing tree, with what seemed to be a door. I opened the door and gasped. I couldn't believe my eyes... a new world. Weirdly wonderful creatures dispersed in fright; dainty nymphs, angry goblins and mischievous elves. 'I come in peace!' I bellowed, quite discombobulated. Is this a dream or is this really happening?

Maya Wood (14)
The Buckingham School, Buckingham

All But One...

There he was... standing there at the end of the rank school corridor, surrounded by all of the pretty cheerleaders. His slicked back, over-gelled hair just covering his gorgeous sapphire eyes. I stood there expectantly waiting. A thought sprung to mind. That small worry started to drown me in fear, so I did what any girl would do in my chain of thought, I started to slowly turn to leave when... I felt a firm grip on my shoulder. 'Wait.' Grimacing. With nerves, I glanced round, it was him... The man I had tried to avoid for so long.

Kizzy Wells (12)
The Buckingham School, Buckingham

Welcome To Wonderland

She stumbled through the woods, tripping over twigs and rocks, surrounded by tall trees soaring through the sky, the broad branches and leaves like lilypads cancel out any possible beam of light to provide a passageway through the mystical forest. A shimmering flash walked past the lost girl and guided her to a swerving path that was lit up by weirdly wonderful fireflies covered head to toe in magenta. Anywhere she looked there were shards of towering grass, sharp enough to cut you, surrounding her. Suddenly, an elf skipped across the path and vanished.

Keeva Audreyann Bennett (14)
The Buckingham School, Buckingham

That Night

Arriving at the carnival, I exited the car and slammed the door shut. Peering through the mirror in the distance, there was a tall, black, mysterious figure watching me. I turned my head and peered over my shoulder to see there was nothing there. At this point, I could feel the hairs on the back of my neck straightening out and a cold shiver ran down my back. As I walked towards the carnival the smell of food overwhelmed me. Now running, I turned a corner and crashed. I wasn't prepared for what would come next; a life-changing experience.

Faye Barber (12)
The Buckingham School, Buckingham

Alice In Wonderland - Gone Wrong!

Alice crawled through the overgrown forest of leaves and sticks, blood dripping from the side of her head. She staggered to her feet and screamed for the Hatter, but her scream was more like a whisper, just reaching the old birch tree in front of her. She called again, but still no reply. Then she heard something; a kind of low growling. Then the ground started to shake. And the growling kept getting louder. Alice, trembling from head to toe, looked up and saw it. The Jabberwocky. And there, in its mouth, with one leg missing, was the Mad Hatter.

Tom Green (13)
The Buckingham School, Buckingham

Welcome To Wonderland

A long day had passed. The sky started becoming stars and eventually all was silent. She slipped into her warm, cosy, comforting bed and drifted away to the place where we all wish we could go: a dream. But was it? She found herself standing alone in an empty room. Suddenly, an oak wood door appeared with a gold lock and handle. She slowly walked towards the door and reached out to open it but before she could, the door opened. A bright light behind her and a strange animal-like figure appeared before her and said... 'Welcome to Wonderland.'

Jessica Emily Cook (14)
The Buckingham School, Buckingham

Runaway Victim

My story is my experience of running away. No one cared about me so I left.

About nine weeks later still I hadn't seen any 'missing' posters. After my uncle's death, my whole family had faded out of my life. Everything happened so fast it was all a blur. All I remember was my uncle shouting at me to run! I ran for my life. All blame came down on me, it was my fault he died. I obviously wasn't wanted so now I'm homeless living in a bus shelter with nothing. That's my story, now it's my life.

Millie Jessopp (12)
The Buckingham School, Buckingham

A Country On The Moon

Shalbainia, a country on the moon. When the comet hit the world that wiped out the dinosaurs, it took some cells and then the comet hit the moon. The comet managed to disperse the cells into a crater. The cells evolved like the cells on Earth, creating humans and a place for them to live. They have water, food, grass, animals and clouds. The only slight difference is there is no gravity so everyone is flying. Shalbainia, a country on the moon just as evolved as England with a currency, trees, rivers, roads, houses and rain. All on the moon!

Rowan Mary Cyster (12)
The Buckingham School, Buckingham

Welcome To Wonderland

My breathing gets heavier and my head throbs. I keep running, running desperately for my life. My footsteps echo behind me, but as do the man's. His footsteps become louder, until I feel him breathing down my neck. He swings his crowbar and I duck my head. The man trips me up and I fall, sprawling onto the forest floor. I try to crawl away, but the man clicks his fingers and the trees around me branch out and restrain me. I scream but the man bends down and puts a finger to my mouth. 'Welcome to Wonderland,' he exclaims.

Sophia Tomes (13)
The Buckingham School, Buckingham

A Stroll In The Woods

Here I am, taking a leisurely stroll in the woods. This is so nice. *Crunch!* What's that? *Snap!* I look around, heart thumping. I hear the sound of birds flapping and squawking. I stare into the abyss. Darkness all around. Bushes are rustling as I walk hesitantly through the forest, on the mossy floor. The wind brushes past my feet, it makes leaves fly by my hair. I stand still for a moment. Bad move. I hear breaths that are not my own. I pick up the pace. I'm now sprinting. My foot catches on a tree root. Oh no!

Rhianna Yardley (13)

The Buckingham School, Buckingham

Lost But Never Found

It was practically silent, all you could hear was the soft, gentle wind. There were only two boys that didn't know where to go, apart from the gigantic mound. All there was to be seen was the ruins of what was left of their old town. The boys sat in silence, not a word to be spoken. The trees were dying, leaves were slowly disappearing and if you were to see those boys you would say they were lost, but never found. This was what the war had caused. Devastation! To every person in the entire universe. Surviving was impossible.

Eve Maia Braddock (12)
The Buckingham School, Buckingham

Welcome To Wonderland

Wonderland: a place many people think of as a place full of sparkling trees and raining sweets like bubblegum, but then why is it that every time I close my eyes and try to see it, it always changes quickly to a place full of hatred and depression? The trees are dead, the rain turns black and has a bitter taste. The people disappear as if humanity never existed except for me.

Why... Maybe because I'm depressed? Or could it be because I can't breathe? I'm cold and when I open my eyes all I can see is black.

Vanesa Vaivadaite (14)

The Buckingham School, Buckingham

The Late-Night Snack

I place it in the oven with my empty stomach. That rich Cornish pasty was made up with meat, steak and potato - oh what I desire most! Slow cooked for pure perfection. Only two hours to go until world peace is achieved. Plate scrubbed hard to make it 100% clear of all bacteria and my cutlery razor-sharp. Well, put it this way my spoon would be a one-hit wonder. Ready, Christmas truly did come early for one lucky small boy. It looked like a heaven-sent angel on a fruitfully white round edged plate. Cornish pasty, thank you. Bye.

Daniel Bunyan (12)
The Buckingham School, Buckingham

The Mistake

Both angry, a couple had a row; a normal thing for them but this time Jackie and Tim had messed it up... big time. This was all in the future so they had a chance to change but there was no point. Jackie was so shocked, she stormed out onto the road and screeched, 'We're over!' But she didn't see the double-decker bus coming her way, getting closer! *Bang*, Tim waits with guilt as he sees his ex on the concrete. They really had messed up. Now, all Tim could do was wait for the sirens to come closer.

Sophie Melluish (12)
The Buckingham School, Buckingham

Welcome To Wonderland

As she placed her pale skin onto the dreamy sofa, she drifted into a sweet slumber. But she woke up seconds later, she wasn't lying on the sofa; she was lying on a soft, white pillow. It looked similar to candyfloss. It was unfamiliar to her. Then she realised where she was. She looked up at the blue sky and then into the blinding sun. When she looked to her right, the silky, white blanket never ended. She was in the clouds. How did she get up there? Suddenly, the clouds began to split. She screamed and began to fall...

Izzy Hardy (14)
The Buckingham School, Buckingham

Dlrow: Backwards Land

Today I saw the most shocking thing, my poor little eyes have ever witnessed. It was out of this dlrow, no, out of this esrevinu. Literally. I started my usual day, it was dark outside, I put my trousers on my arms and my top on my legs. Suddenly, outside my window, lights flashed, and a creature popped out of the nowhere. He looked like me, but did everything different. He walked on his feet, instead of his hands, he wears his clothes the wrong way round and he wore a skirt instead of trousers. I still cannot believe it!

Sophie Knight (12)
The Buckingham School, Buckingham

Wonderland Gone Wrong

Trees' fingers grab my throbbing ankles as I hang upside down, looking down at the meandering stream. My nose tingles as flies buzz around my flaring nostrils. Suddenly, the trees' fingers discard my ankles and I swing to the side of the stream, landing in the undergrowth which starts pulling me down, down beneath the soil. As I open my mouth to breathe, all I can taste is dirt and what I presume to be a slimy-skinned worm. This must be the end, I know it, no one can help me now, so much for a nice family holiday.

Megan Drew (12)
The Buckingham School, Buckingham

The Wonder World

There was a place far from Earth, nothing like Earth. Not a single bit like Earth. The sky is green, there are four moons. They're orange, purple, red and blue. Me. Only me. On this lonely wonder world. Here I roam freely by myself. But I stop still. The floor suddenly starts cracking and shaking. But it's OK, I see in the distance a herd of menacing birds. I look up and the sky is ferocious. Suddenly, I find myself falling in outer space. I think I'm going to die. With a bang, I land on the floor. Back home.

Ellie-Mae Harfield (12)
The Buckingham School, Buckingham

My Life

I was nine. Only nine. It was frightening. I had pains in my chest. So I found out I had ASD. It is a heart disease and my world was destroyed. In September 2016 I had open heart surgery and I was petrified. Looking at the clock time after time, I finally went for the operation. But it's all over now and I am trying to help others. I felt lost but I got through it. I have family and friends, that's what matters. That's my story. That's my fight. That's my life. It's me. My heart is fixed. Yay.

Aimee Rous (12)
The Buckingham School, Buckingham

The Secret Is Out

The scream was immense. It echoed, creating ripples on the musty river. News travels fast, and the search began. He's still out there and so is she. Or so they thought. Everyone has hope, they think they can find her, but I know the truth. I know what happened that night. This is her story, Cindy. I know how he did it. I know where he hid the body. It has ruled me, keeping the secret, so I am telling you. If tomorrow I'm gone, look in the bottom of the musty river... I'll be there and so will Cindy.

Summer Jones (12)
The Buckingham School, Buckingham

Never Alone

Footsteps. Clock chimes. *Tick. Tock. Clip. Clop.* As I walk down these cold, isolated corridors, fear creeps up on me like a ghost, haunting me till the day I die. Which way do I go? All I do is shake, as I try to find a way out. But how? And where? And when? My heart began to race. *Boom! Boom! Boom!* I count the time it takes, the steps I have walked. Gazing around the deserted hall, I just want to leave. A gust of wind rushes the room. Someone else is here. I am not alone any more...

Lily-Mae Cross (12)
The Buckingham School, Buckingham

Trapped...

I was staring into the dark mist, forcing my hand to reach and open the door, or what was left of a door. Nobody seemed to come here and I felt a shiver down my spine. When the door opened, I felt like I was going to fall through the old and uneven floorboards. I take a step forward... My heart trembling and racing! Blood splattered up the wall, I look down, a body... a dead body! I ran as fast as I could, circling round and round, banging on every ruined door. Body slowly fainting, I was trapped...

Sinead O'Neill (13)
The Buckingham School, Buckingham

All Alone

I was sat there. All alone. No one was anywhere. Covered, surrounded by tall towering trees. What should I do? I can see no way out. I am stuck. I must think fast. Around me I can see three sticks, four twigs and grass. Lots of grass. What could I build with that? I could try and make a stool. A step of some sort. To lift me to the tree so I could climb high, high above the trees so maybe I could escape. Escape from the wild! Escape from this. Is that really too hard to ask for?

Harriet Cahill (13)
The Buckingham School, Buckingham

Reality Vs The Remaining One

Diseased, I awake from cocooning under my duvet.
Nothing, I hear nothing. Trembling, I creep carefully
downstairs. It's abandoned. Where are my parents? They've
disappeared. It's weird. Half my vision is focused on
our happy life, whereas my other half, the world
is disorientated and lonely.
My parents gently welcome me and offer me food. Yet
everywhere I walk I hear a wicked noise. The abandoned
area intrigues me, notes cover the tattered wall. It tells me,
'Come up!' Left foot first and right behind, I cautiously peek
my head around the corner and to my surprise there is...

Amelia Summerton (13)

The Vale Academy, Brigg

Aerth

The buzz of crawling insects, overwhelmed senses; air as thick as a brick wall. I'm in the rainforest. I feel alone, and now every shadow is a jaguar, every leaf a threat. But I wasn't wrong to be paranoid...

Suddenly, the blanket of trees is filled with ground-breaking beasts. Some happily munching plants, plodding along, slow and sleepy - some with the intention of murder. Some with rippling muscles, skin like leather, legs the size of tree trunks, rows of blade-like fangs. Dinosaurs.

Swarming tribal people, in threatening streaks of war paint, surround me. 'Welcome to Wonderland,' they say.

Amy Taylor (12)
The Vale Academy, Brigg

Animal Kingdom Afterlife

My name's Jon Kruson, I was diagnosed with depression two years ago, and this is where I ended it all...
I awoke, I didn't think Heaven was real, but here I am. It's an oasis, luscious with plants, animals everywhere. I approach one of the animals. 'Back off!' the lion grumbled.
'How can you talk?' I replied.
'We evolved, in afterlife we evolve,' he says, as if I'm stupid. Bewildered, I fall to the ground, sitting with my back hunched forward. I can only form two clear thoughts: *What happened to all the humans, and is this Heaven or Hell?*

Thomas Hewis
The Vale Academy, Brigg

Sweetopyse Land

This land is away from everything... At midday, the visitor explored. He found sweets, sweets and more sweets: there were houses, factories and machines made from sweets. 'T-t-t-this is a mystery,' he said. First, he met strange candy creatures. They said, 'This has been here for ten years and there had been a great success.' The first visitor ever to go there was this one; he had a very entertaining day. These strange creatures performed a dance and the visitor collected lots of sweets and candy from these creatures. However, then they all surrounded him and suddenly...

Shannon Pearson (11)

The Vale Academy, Brigg

Don't Fall Down

It swallowed me whole. Falling. Falling. *Thud!* I pelted the bottom. Dazed, hurt, confused. I brought myself to my feet like a newborn lamb. I looked around, trenches? Hold on, I learnt about this in history. I was in the middle of a battlefield in World War One.

Over in the distance, there was some kind of giant lathered in jewellery, diamonds and gems. Hang on, that's Henry VIII. What! He's a Tudor... and, *bang!* He collapsed. The soldiers took aim again and the ripple of machine gun fire rang round my ears, and then my head... blood? Black...

Adam Skinn

The Vale Academy, Brigg

The War-Torn, Endless Supernova

Bang! Woah, what happened... I stepped out into the unknown, not recognising my own home town. Stood before me were corpses that littered the pavement and destroyed buildings. I didn't know what to do until I stumbled upon a hole...

There I was, potentially falling to my death via an abyss. *Phew!* That was one of the most intense things I've done before; I just got spurted out of an underwater volcano, into an endless ocean. Where am I? What am I doing here? How am I going to survive? These are just a few words spiralling around my head.

Aisling Skye Ellis (12)

The Vale Academy, Brigg

Unhappy Endings

'Run! Run till you can run no more! That thing is still behind you!'

I awoke, reliving the trauma from the last days. I left the room and walked the broken streets, alone. Something caught my eye. I ignored it and stared blankly at a mirror, hoping to find someone I'd lost: myself. This place was haunting. Icy wind crashed around me. Something stumbled my way. I saw it, a black cat, and managed to smile, something I thought I'd lost. 'I see you.'

A cold, tinny voice, not myself, from nobody I could see replied, 'I see you too.'

Poppy May Merrifield (13)

The Vale Academy, Brigg

Strange

I took a deep breath, as I felt my heart beat against my chest sweat dripped from my forehead due to the sweltering heat. 'Where are we?' I questioned, hoping for an answer.

'The future,' answered Thomas. I could just make out London's landmarks, Big Ben (half-destroyed, the clock still ticking), the Eye (toppled over, missing carriages) and the HOP (burning). We wandered through the streets ,searching for somewhere to eat or drink and then it happened. From over the collapsed Eye, a herd of creatures charged, we ran for our lives...

Charlie Robinson (12)

The Vale Academy, Brigg

Portam

Maria was fed up; Mother and Father were arguing again, and baby brother, Charlie, was crying. Father had told Maria many times, 'Stay away from the gate.' However, before she knew it, she found herself in front of it. Was it to prove she'd had enough of them arguing? Maria slowly walked through the gate and into the forest. *Snap!* She broke a twig beneath her feet; the trees were groaning, leaves whispering. Maria decided to turn back, however something was holding her back. Was it her conscience? No! She looked down at her feet...

Georgia Tock (11)
The Vale Academy, Brigg

Satan's Kingdom

They woke up, not knowing where they were, clueless about anything around them. It was Hell. Rocks and molten lava everywhere. They needed to find a way out. They only had food and drink in their bags. There were two children, a mum and dad. After miles of looking for anything, they failed. Two super volcanoes and an asteroid affected the world at the same time. They were in Satan's kingdom. They needed to escape. Luckily, there was a scrapyard with enough materials to build a rocket ship. They could get out. They did... to a whole different, better world.

Jake Houghton (11)
The Vale Academy, Brigg

Trapped In Dream City

Another day in Dream City, yet everything was about to change... Maddie stepped towards the portal, she was a dreamer, meaning she is one of the people that can only go through the portal to Dream City. Only this time, she brought her best friend, Brynn. But Brynn wasn't a dreamer; she was normal, although she could only go through the portal if a dreamer was with her. The two girls explored the wonderful city, but there was a problem. Normal people like Brynn can't get back out. Little did they know, Brynn was trapped in Dream City forever.

Hannah Shearwood (12)

The Vale Academy, Brigg

After A Dream

Carefully, I glided up the mysterious, almost candyfloss staircase; gazing at disappearing trees and listening to the silence. This cloud built up, making a castle-like shape. Here there wouldn't be any shouting. It's almost soulless. Just me and a lovely woman who looks like my mother used to. I can just play by myself in a room full of toys; when I get tired, the woman can squeeze me tight (like a parent and baby) whilst she sings a lullaby. My eyes opened, hearing shouting. The innkeeper, a devil! Why can't life be a castle on a cloud?

Charlotte Clark (13)
The Vale Academy, Brigg

Uncharted

Terrified, petrified and horrified, Steven ran for his life, trying to get away from a pack of wild dire wolves. He fell. Everything went black. This was how it happened. Steven went exploring into the woods, like he normally did to find his tree house. When suddenly, he fell into a hole that led to a room with a glowing red orb that called his name. Steven touched the orb and in a flash of light he got transported to the world of uncharted. Terrified, petrified and horrified, Steven ran for his dear life. He fell. Everything went black, uncharted.

Alex Atkinson (12)
The Vale Academy, Brigg

The Unknown Tomorrow

Adrenaline pumped through my shivering body, as if I was an athlete ready to launch off blocks. Into the shadowed corner of my eye there rose a vicious, menacing figure, blazing blood dripping from its unforgiving teeth, claws as sharp as razors and of course a mind set crazy like a clown! I was trapped inside a war, a crisis, all I knew was that I felt unwanted on the verge of becoming a forgotten soul, in a world where government was gone. Whether I'd live another day, hour, minute was ominous. Would tomorrow tell a different tale?

Thomas Armstrong (13)
The Vale Academy, Brigg

The City Of Danger

The fresh smell of blood floats in the air, with the gore of human remains lying on the streets, scattered in a city of danger. Every day, more and more people go, leaving more people crying for their lost ones, only to be slaughtered by those haunting, most despicable creatures. Those nightmares. Those world destroyers.

Our tribe seeks for hope, for one day the fearing of death will no longer bother us, but until then we hide in the back alleys of the blackened-out streets, hiding from the monsters that look for us. The zombies!

Ross Smith (13)

The Vale Academy, Brigg

The Lone Dweller

I was five when the bombs first dropped, the sound of the sirens was deafening and the blinding flash of the detonation told me I needed to run. Somehow I made it to the shelter but it was just me, alone.

I am fifteen now and it has been a difficult ten years, my Geiger counter in the roof shows the radiation is at a safe level. I decide it is time. The hatch slowly creaks open and the murky light pours in. I cautiously step out onto the barren wasteland and then I see it, something I won't forget...

Euan Hall (12)

The Vale Academy, Brigg

Coldness, Darkness... Silence

It's cold, but the sun shines. It's dark and starry and blurry but it's daytime. Vision and pain - gone. No feeling. I know it's death pulling me into its grasp. The curse of 2049.. Ha! I've cheated death - that precious bottle on the marble worktop. An antidote. The money I can prise out of the rich to pay for a precious sip to save them from death. The money! I pulled across the curtain and quickly pulled it shut again. A corpse was there - mouth open in a silent scream for a sip of the antidote.

Tom Nightingale (11)

The Vale Academy, Brigg

Dreaming Monsters

He awoke to the sound of an army retreating, or was it an army? At that moment, Jake's friend, Percy, rushed into the strange room he had been put in. Jake rose and walked past him into the street, only to find that he was on a bridge in Manhattan, and that he had come out of a tent! Then he remembered, he must have been knocked out because seconds ago he was fighting a monster army. Now, he was staring at mounds of monster essence. The remains of them in the mortal world, since they had returned to Tartarus.

James Goude (11)

The Vale Academy, Brigg

Never Leaving

I stood still. I was frozen. I couldn't believe where I was. I slowly looked up, my whole body was trembling. I'd been locked in. Behind me I could hear deep footsteps. Suddenly, I was being pushed into a gigantic, dark wooden castle. Full of wizards and magical creatures. 'In bed before six! Only don't leave the castle before 11am!'

There were so many rules people were shouting and screaming at me. I hated it, I hated it. i just wanted it to stop. I wanted to leave. Help me!

Abbie Lammiman (12)
The Vale Academy, Brigg

Love Caused By An Apocalypse

I'd awoken from my sleep and still felt drowsy. I stood up, I stumbled to the window of my bedroom and gazed into the distance. I couldn't make out what the figure coming towards my house was, due to the fog. After a while, I finally managed to work out the strange silhouette; it wasn't good. I couldn't believe my eyes; it was a zombie. I thought it was going to kill me until a woman pounced onto it and stopped it. I let her in, she said that her name was Sue, I knew her from somewhere...

Archie Williamson (12)
The Vale Academy, Brigg

My Favourite Day

Today is my favourite day. If you don't know the standard prison talk, my favourite day is the riot day. You know the one that they march in and invade your cell. I swear they just do it to pass time that goes by in here.

I start to smother myself in baby oil, I rip a pole from my bed ready for the wasps to swarm in. The adrenaline trickles through my body when I hear the key turning in the complicated lock. 'Stand and face the back wall!' It happens in slow motion.

Freya Watson (12)
The Vale Academy, Brigg

War!

James was shaking. He was in a dirty, rat-infested trench. Corpses were littered everywhere. *Boom. Crash. Bang.* 'There goes another few soldiers,' I sighed. Between us and the enemy is a land where it's like a painting, if the trees weren't swaying, then it would be.

This war-torn place was filled with fears, everything was decrepit. This town looked wrecked. Will this place become pleasant or will it still stay decrepit? This is a bad, nebulous place to be!

Oliver Whitaker (12)
The Vale Academy, Brigg

Chuttely Boop!

I was left in this horrible place! My mum had dumped me here, the room was full of sweets - it made me feel nauseous! There are kids everywhere barging their way to Mount Marshmallowia. Thinking to myself, I realised it was some sort of place where you dumped your kids and never got them back! A girl just came up to me and patted me on the back and smiled. Obviously, I smiled back (not wanting to be rude) but she just laughed. Then I saw her spotty face with black teeth (eeew!).

Selena May Capp (11)

The Vale Academy, Brigg

A Slave To Labour

Walls fall and tunnels crumble, slave workers always tumble. Their clothes are ripped and torn, the workers always left to mourn. They are left in the mine with no importance. Our life, our homes come to nothing. We all starve in the mist, coughing. People die every day, moving further and further away. As we sleep through the silent breathing night, the echoes of the tunnels haunt us saying goodnight. Our feet are cold and cut as we sleep, our mouths tie shut.

Jake Forman (12)
The Vale Academy, Brigg

Seatopia

One blink, and it was gone. At first I thought I had washed up on shore, but I gradually began to realise I hadn't. The sea was gone. But where had everybody gone? I stood, on my own, my heart racing out of my chest, sweat flowing down my face onto the hot sand. The darkness. A howling sound from behind got louder and louder until it felt like it was inside me. All of a sudden, I was falling through the sky, the wind blowing my hair back. Then...

Casey Griffin (12)
The Vale Academy, Brigg

Mysterious Hand

Time stood still. My heart raced and I froze. Fear had faced me in the eyes. I can still hear the scratches of the knife running across the floor. I slowly stood up, even though I was in so much pain. I nervously (as the intruder left the door open) walked to the phone. Suddenly, a cold, big hand grabbed me from behind. I fell to the dusty, hard floor again for the second time, but this time I didn't get up...

Faith Elizabeth Cavill (12)

The Vale Academy, Brigg

Darkness

Darkness. Darkness is what I woke up to. Before all this happened, it was okay. Every day, every minute, I see my friends in pain, missing the old days. Now, as we look outside, we see all the dead, walking corpses. Gormless, clueless. The only thing they know is that we are prey. They want our flesh; our red blood. And we know that one day... we will be hunted. One day it'll all be over; we will be one of them.

Katie Johnson (12)

The Vale Academy, Brigg

A Cat-Astrophic Event

Have you ever heard of zombies? If you have not, you have been living under a rock... This is a story about zombies... Cat zombies!

In a fur, furaway land, the angry zombie cats are having a conversation:

'The missiles are being deployed meow-ster!' said Kitty Purry.

'Purr-fect,' said Lucifurr, king of the zombie cats. 'Three hours two minutes has passed since the zombie outbreak, do you know what this means?' screeched Lucifurr to Leopawdo Dicatrio.

'Yes, we need to stay paw-sitive in this claw-full situation and purr-haps keep your hunger under control!'

'Are you furr-eal?' exclaimed Lucifurr.

Cerys Vernon (13)
Ysgol Gyfun Llangefni, Llangefni

When You Go Down To The Woods Today...

Luna strolled into the woods, holding the lead attached to her dog, Albus. Luna decided to release Albus and let him wander around. As her companion explored the surrounding area, Luna went in search of a stick to throw for him. She eventually came across a long twig which looked as if it had been polished. Luna bent over to pick it up whilst Albus looked ready to go and fetch it. She threw the stick when something unexpected happened! Golden sparks flew out of the tip of the stick. She had found a magic wand!

Mia Pritchard Evans (14)

Ysgol Gyfun Llangefni, Llangefni

2054

Death lingers amongst this cruel planet. Helpless children drag themselves along forgotten streets, thin as mist and expressionless. Abandoned on doorsteps, vulnerable babies whimper for their mothers, scrawled letters for adoption clenched in their tiny fists. Departing from another day at the factories, nonchalant men wearily shuffle past without a backward glance, their hearts as cold as ice. Defenceless women work as slaves, the history of female rights long relinquished. Brown tendrils of smoke and pollution fill the atmosphere; nobody knows the real colour of the sky. Dense fog swirls around crumbling buildings, cloaking their decaying structures. Welcome to Earth.

Ella Wintle (12)

Ysgol Y Preseli, Crymych

The New Beginning

Eve stumbled over a jagged piece of metal. Surprised, she carefully picked it up, only to find carved writing inside, stating 'courtesy of the Death Eaters'. Suddenly, her mind was flooded with memories of the war. She burst out crying. Tearfully, she remembered her mother's words, 'Stay alive my darling, stay alive.' Determined, she surveyed the barren landscape, searching in every nook and cranny for any signs of life. She hadn't seen another human for months. Exhausted, she looked for food. She snuck through a crumbling building, frantically searching for anything edible. Unexpectedly, a voice shouted, 'What do you want?'

Olivia Dobney (11)
Ysgol Y Preseli, Crymych

Perfect Pain

Perfect. It's too perfect. Chirping, the birds fly across the blue sky. And with the neighbour's welcoming cheer I feel the warm breeze around me, but something's just not right. The neighbours show me what's left of their happy past, now their soul has disappeared and pain controls. Black clouds swarm their lives, terror is their only living feeling, slowly they are being swallowed by this monster, this vigorous, formidable rage is killing them. They're trapped in a cage of their own misery. Fading rapidly, their last hope of freedom is scarce. Goodbye, good riddance. Good luck. Welcome to Wonderland.

Brooke Amy Evans-Harries (12)
Ysgol Y Preseli, Crymych

Athena

Athena knew this day would come, but not this soon. An acrid taste pierced Athena's throat... Guilt... She knew this would happen but kept it to herself. Illuminous orange vines started growing uncontrollably. People started panicking, there was always order, the same thing happened daily. Evacuation was taking place, but the vines followed. Athena knew that no one would survive. Vines would become poisonous soon. Her heart started pounding. How could she survive? There was only one answer. She wouldn't. She had no other choice but to breathe. She tried to hold her breath but failed. Suddenly, she felt faint...

Angharad Jones (12)
Ysgol Y Preseli, Crymych

The Nightmare

This is not fear. Fear is an emotion people get when they're frightened, but this... This is something no human should feel, something that makes dying and going to Hell very appealing. 'Just give in,' Nightmare said. 'Die and you let me into the real world, then you will be free of me. We'll both be happy.'

'No!' I screamed. 'That can't happen!'

At that, Nightmare showed me something horrible. I saw my parents, sinking to the ground, skin melting, the image terrifyingly vivid. I screamed so loud my throat burned. I sank to the floor and I gave in.

Will Parrott (12)

Ysgol Y Preseli, Crymych

Beneath

Splash! The plane hit the water at full speed, taking all passengers with it. The plane was fine, no deaths, no cracks, nothing. Tumbling out, everyone was fine, the mirror land was expanding. Everything was as it was, just more colourful and wavy, something wasn't right. Planes were coming down every second, darkness was on the horizon, urging closer as every plane came down. Planes came down, quicker, darkness gaining. 'Run, everyone run!' They took the warning and tried to sprint away. They went nowhere. Darkness was at finger's reach. They all vanished into thin air...

Iolo Griffiths (12)

Ysgol Y Preseli, Crymych

The Last Breath

Vladimir opened his eyes to see destruction everywhere, pieces of stone were crashing on the floor. The meteor rain was giving out tremendous sound. Everyone screaming for hope to save their lives. Suddenly, Vladimir was hit by a meteor. Struggling to save his life, he looked around to see what was happening, everywhere he looked he saw flaming, hot fireballs scattering across the area. Fire burnt everything living and non-living. This was the end, there was no chance he'd survive. Nothing would still be intact. With his one final breath he hoped things would be better in the next life.

Steffan Thomas (12)
Ysgol Y Preseli, Crymych

The Peaceful Mystery

Dancing high above Earth, there's a beautiful planet, a planet so extraordinary that all mythical creatures live there, from unique little unicorns to big mighty dragons. But they all live in peace. Animals like horses and tigers live there, almost all the nearly extinct or endangered animals live there. It was a peaceful place and there was grass as far as the eye can see. The weather was always wonderful and there was always food, water and shelter for these lucky creatures. There was no ruler, they were happy just the way life was. But then the horrible disaster happened!

Freya Watkins-Williams (11)

Ysgol Y Preseli, Crymych

Unknown World

It had all changed, everything was different. I could never imagine blossom trees quivering in the wind, all of it was gone. Dead corpses cloaked the ground and separated light from darkness, Centaurs guarded the gate to their land of wonder. I peered through the gate, closed one eye; sorrow, that's what I saw underneath his apple skin. Struggling, the man tried connecting objects together. It was shaped like a cylinder and had booming flashing lights around it. He operated the control system. 'Goodbye world,' he whispered. What did he mean? What was happening?

Nell Evans (11)
Ysgol Y Preseli, Crymych

Rivalry Destroys The Kingdom

Into the depths of the big, blue sea, the kingdom of devils roamed with their fierce spears and razor-sharp horns. Endless fighting haunted the kingdom. But one day, something shocked the kingdom. Two devils had been brewing a rivalry for decades - Zogel and Amptious. Coincidentally, they both met at a shop containing deadly weapons! Amptious reached out for the deadliest spear in the world. He launched the spear with power at Zogel, but narrowly missed and glided through the king of the kingdom! Amptious was sent to the tower where he was executed. The kingdom wasn't the same after!

Evan Watts (12)

Ysgol Y Preseli, Crymych

My Dying Wonderland

Empty. Hollow. Cold. Light flickered from the burning candles. Deserted houses lay rotting in mud. Walking through, I shivered at the sight of dead corpses. Silence tore through me like a blade through butter. Suddenly, a sharp whistle was blown. War was upon this once peaceful land. A minefield. Thundering across the fields were knights on their almighty horses. I was in the middle of battle. Flaming torches brushed along the dying trees, alighting them. Flames rose like an almighty beast roaring from under. All was being destroyed before my eyes. My heart, my soul, my home. My wonderland.

Mair Wilshaw (12)

Ysgol Y Preseli, Crymych

The City Of The Future

Crash! The hover car went into one of the skyscrapers, glass shards pierced his skin, he was driving away from the murderer he feared. The murderer was chasing him. Tomos knew he had to run. The murderer, holding electrified throwing knives, threw them at Tomos. One went through his arm, he was still driving. Wind blew his hair back, looking back, skyscrapers astronomically high. He was escaping from the city of the future. The murderer was chasing him, Tomos going up all these turns and bends, he was trying to dodge the bullets and buildings, but it was too late...

Thomas William Nicholas (11)

Ysgol Y Preseli, Crymych

The Underworld

He stood there, feeling lonely and nervous simultaneously. The daunting, dark, dangerous alleyways beckoned him in. He took a deep breath, puffed out his chest, and stuttered slowly into the unknown. He glanced up at the sea which he had dropped through. As he carried on through the gloomy darkness, he caught the attention of a mysterious black, shadowy figure. The odd figure muttered something to himself then sprinted towards him with a mangled, twisted knife. He tried to get away but the figure was too fast. Now they were centimetres away, glaring at each other with evil eyes...

Freddy Larsen (11)
Ysgol Y Preseli, Crymych

Over The Rainbow

Sarah tried opening her eyes but the light of that portal she fell through was too blinding. Finally, she was able to see daylight but there wasn't much to see. Darkness clung to her like a blanket over a dying soul. Pollution made it very hard to breathe, she couldn't feel her legs. People were shouting, children were crying, animals bellowing. Footsteps became louder, someone was coming towards her. Opening the door was a tall man with muscles of stone. Suddenly that light appeared again, she was unable to see but she was in a river somewhere over the rainbow.

Ffion Ann Peregrine (12)
Ysgol Y Preseli, Crymych

Pool Of Crystal Tears

I'm being filmed for video game footage, against my will. My heart is pounding in my chest. It's practically exploding. Failure is not an option. I leap, stretching as far as I can, across the fiery pools of lava. Fierce, smouldering flickers of flames are licking the air around me. Cameras are peering down on me. These people are corrupted in the mind! I've made it through to the next biome. Glistening, shimmering pools of crystal tears are everywhere. I'm in awe. I touch the nearest one, it transforms into pits of acid darkness. It's consuming me into the abyss!

Catrin Bishop (12)
Ysgol Y Preseli, Crymych

Delighted

Why am I here? Do I belong here? Dan thought to himself, *Why am I in such a phenomenal place?* Smooth, shiny glass buildings tower into the white, fluffy clouds. I stood like a solid statue as my eyes stared at the amazing buildings. Slowly I started sneaking around as I rapidly scanned the whole land. I was delighted as I watched the young children play on the bright, shiny, green, beautiful grass. 'Dan, are you OK?' my brother James asked. It took me a while to reply. Everything was blocked out. 'Yes,' I said. My adventure had just begun.

Erin Rees-James (12)

Ysgol Y Preseli, Crymych

Burning Space

Bright, flashing in the deep dark, but glistening in space. Mystical. Tom took a leap, while dreaming of home. He couldn't go back. Suddenly, Tom could see the stars which reminded him of the hellhole. His home. Drifting on top of his confused head, Tom clutched his freezing, dead legs. Swiftly cruising, he floated while moving to the sun. Glistening in the pitch-black air, Tom could see the spiteful sun burning all the poor, innocent stars. Tom was metres away from the sun. He gradually inched his way to the malicious devil. Would he survive? Who knows the truth?

Manon John (11)

Ysgol Y Preseli, Crymych

The Unknown Battle

Bright sunlight sparkles on one side and flames rise on the other. Each side ruled by powerful people. One side contains light, happiness and joy but the other contains darkness, misery and pain.

One day the dark side was becoming stronger and more powerful and many were killed. After killing many, the psycho demon and the powerful god came face-to-face. The demon and the god battled and fought for victory. The split personality planet was destroyed and all living creatures died. The winner of the battle is still anonymous and nobody will ever know who won the fight.

Jemma Pinkney (12)
Ysgol Y Preseli, Crymych

Almost There, Almost To Nothing

The sign read, *Welcome To Wonderland* but darkness swam through the thickness of the pollution and obscured my hopeful thoughts of how close I was to the city. I took a tentative step towards the place I had once called home. A bomb erupted inside my body where my heart was supposed to be as the shock of my view took over my entire brain. Skyscrapers blocked any wisps of light attempting to break through. Fog and pollution worked together, watching over the deadly silence. This wasn't right, but it was evidence that there was someone or something out there!

Hetty Lort-Phillips (12)

Ysgol Y Preseli, Crymych

The Battle To End All

Hand in hand, the brothers stood, suspicious of when the enemy would strike! Cries and screams were ringing of the warrior's children. It became obvious that it was time, this was it! The be all or end all. Suddenly, an arrow flew past me, the battle had begun. Charging towards the rotten Romans in rage. It was a very gruesome battle and bloody too, with a very restricted vision, the smoke was extremely thick and brought a silence to the battle. The smoke rapidly disappeared and left many in a horrific state, seeing their companions lay dead on the floor.

Ifan Thomas (12)

Ysgol Y Preseli, Crymych

It's Not Easy

You'd think being a fox in a paradise like Aasonia would be easy, but it's not. There's picking up the kids from playgroup and then keeping them quiet in the hovercar whilst trying not to hit a tree crossing the road, and don't get me started on work. Argh! Looking after a garden centre is extremely hard. I have to make sure that families like the Oaks and the Pines choose the right family tree, and families like the Daisys and the Hyacinths choose the right house. The only good thing is that people don't hunt us foxes any more.

Sophie Louise Philipsen (14)

Ysgol Y Preseli, Crymych

Into The Blue

She dived into the crystal waters, turning into a mythical creature. Her long smooth hair flowed in the ocean. Her beautiful, glimmery, aqua-blue tail swished. The rocks were pumice-grey, like a volcano on a calamitous day. Different colours and sizes were the spiky corals. Speaking to the animals such as the pouncing dolphins and the silent seahorse, she found all sorts of treasures - gold, silver, bronze and some aqua too. The warmth of the sun she felt on her tail. The dampness on her tail was very soothing and refreshing. What a wondrous wet wonderland.

Seren Lewis (11)
Ysgol Y Preseli, Crymych

Cursed

Every day is the same, everyone fits in. Apart from me. I'm Sophie, I live in Erudite, a dark, miserable, bleak, soulless place. Where every day is the same; wake up, feed chickens, go to school, home, and go to bed. We are cursed by an Enchantress to live every day the same. Our country became greedy, jealous, ungrateful. Now we have nothing. The darkness invades our land like the plague. Pollution destroys the nature we have left. The air is no longer pure. Happiness is no longer a word in our vocabulary. I plan on changing all of that...

Ruby Emma Travis (11)
Ysgol Y Preseli, Crymych

Lost In The Unknown

Suddenly, I wasn't at all sure where I was, all around fragments of charcoal and shards of glass fell from the sky. Not a whisper of light gazed on the surface. What was happening? I didn't belong here. Staring into the distance, I wondered how I would be able to return home. In the corner of my eye, someone or something scrambled across the cobbled road through the gloomy, thick air. Gasping at the sight, I crept silently behind the back of a wall. Suddenly, a flicker of light exploded into the air and there they stood. 'Who are you?'

Seren Rees (11)

Ysgol Y Preseli, Crymych

Cameras And Bots

'The cameras, they're watching us,' whispered Beth, she was obviously just as scared as I was. We crept out from the shadows, looking out for anything that could possibly be a search bot. Crime, a crime could be your downfall, anything from a scratch on a wall, to murder; a crime could seal your fate. 'What had we done?' Those words repeated themselves again and again in my head. One mark on a wall, that's all it took, now the bots were at our throats. We tried to hide, but they caught us, our fate was sealed, or was it?

Efa Gardner (11)
Ysgol Y Preseli, Crymych

The Clown

Silence filled the darkened room as Jack tried not to make a single sound. He knew it was here, his only fear, the clown. His gaze wandered around the room until it settled on a red helium balloon floating on the ceiling. Then he heard a voice, a voice he was strangely drawn towards. It wasn't a voice he recognised. The voice said, 'Come here with me and we can go.' It repeated the phrase a few times more, each time increasing in volume. Then it stopped. He heard footsteps nearing. He remained as still as possible. He looked up...

Ruben Mansfield (13)
Ysgol Y Preseli, Crymych

The Dystopic Life Of A Runaway Girl

Recently, I (Camille), ran away from Phoenix to New York, seeking a better life. This was certainly not the case for me. I've been haunted by a horrifying vision of a city of bones, so I became one of The Circle, dedicated to freedom from this terrible life. Sprinting for the edge, I jumped for the train. They had been looted for the metal a while ago, so it's safe. I have no idea how to help anything here. I've been called to a meeting. Fifteen storeys up, without any hesitation, I jumped and fell a hundred metres straight down...

Katey-Anne Othen (12)

Ysgol Y Preseli, Crymych

The Last Race Of Life

Shards of steel lunged into the air. It had been triggered. He had run. Jim knew it. Sirens bellowed in the background. He was on his way. The journey began. The time was here, police sprinted round the corner. Pouncing into the air, he landed into the bin. Throwing the lid onto the bin - little did he know there was a hungry dog in there. The dog bit him, blood oozed down his leg. He grabbed the dog's neck and strangled him to death. They were there, they found out where he was. He was doomed. Goodbye, the world.

Ben Blewitt (11)

Ysgol Y Preseli, Crymych

World War III

The world is about to end with everyone fighting for their countries as World War III carries on. Many people have died. Trump is the leader of the dangerous team of killers. The British army could send a nuclear bomb to end what Trump started. Nobody knows what has come to this world! Some people say that everyone should stay with their whole family before the end happens. All that stands is rubble and bodies rotting away. The sky is dark and the wind curls through stone houses. The British have a big decision. What should they do now?

Rhys Ouseley (12)
Ysgol Y Preseli, Crymych

The Rise Of Mother Nature

Screaming. Destruction. Corruption. I am Mother Nature. In my wake I have left families heartbroken; hopes and dreams crushed into dust. I watch people fight for their lives, clambering and clawing for a way out. But it's too late. I envelope them in my dark clutches. But for those who have escaped my darkness, I am coming for you. I am Mother Nature. I was born to destroy; I was born to rule. No man can overcome my powers. I have the power of life and death. I am the ruler of this kingdom. I'm the ruler of the world.

Ella Picton-Thomas (13)

Ysgol Y Preseli, Crymych

Astruxias' Assassination

War is coming. This world, a paradise for all, will be destroyed by war. Up to now the world has been peaceful as everyone has got along; now families are far more powerful than in the past, where everything was so simple. I fear that this will signal the end of Astruxias. The world after war will be nothing but rotting human remains, rubble and blown-out tanks. There is no way to escape this deadly war, especially when you are one of the few innocent people left in the world. My time is almost over. War is coming.

Charlotte Caitlin Pickford (13)

Ysgol Y Preseli, Crymych

What Has The World Become?

Trembling, my hand turned the doorknob. The creaking door swung open to reveal the outside world. All the grass was grey and dead. The trees bared no leaves and the grey sky blanketed the colourless world. I was cold. I felt no wind. 'Got to find food.' I managed to squeak through my hunger. The desolate streets which used to be filled with happy people were now completely empty. I found what I was looking for. An abandoned shop. I knew that I was being watched. Would I ever see the warm sun again? What had the world become?

John Griffith (12)

Ysgol Y Preseli, Crymych

The Night Prevails Over The Light

I walked slowly down the stairs. Today was my last day in this dreaded place. My secret husband is coming to collect me from my prison. As my fiance went to the podium to begin to raise our largest sun, a swirl of darkness descended to my side. People around me started to scream as my husband came to stand by my side. He smiled at my shell-shocked fiance. 'Let's leave, my darling,' he said as he placed a hand around my waist and we left to the castle of darkness. The effort drained me and darkness enfolded me.

Niamh Grant (14)

Ysgol Y Preseli, Crymych

Eye Can See You

Staring at the gloomy clouds that ruled the polluted sky, she took one last breath of the cold, dusty air. Linzy knew she wasn't safe, she had to leave. The world was miserable living by the strict eye of the leader. One by one everyone was dying of starvation, no one was safe. The world in a bubble was not a life for her. The clear glass bubble surrounded every view, all she wanted was to be free again. Taking a last look at the place she once called her home, Linzy plunged herself into the darkness of the unknown...

Lowri Pritchard (12)
Ysgol Y Preseli, Crymych

Pangea

Click. I slipped my right hand out of my shackles. I stretched the tender skin on my wrists. These shackles had been on too long. My feet dried in the dust as I slipped in and out of the wooden huts that housed all the slaves. I was going to free my brothers and sisters from this cruel world. I was going to crush this land, send out shockwaves and collapse their petty empire. I slowed to a walk as I reached the top of the hill. I gazed down at the landscape, spread my arms and unleashed the earthquakes.

Maya Oyibo-Goss (14)
Ysgol Y Preseli, Crymych

He Had One

The man gripped his gun as he crawled through undergrowth. Suddenly, he heard the unmistakable sound of a twig cracking. They were onto him. He got up and sprinted away. He heard gunfire behind him and saw the bullets thud into the trees beside him. He zigzagged and dived into the river. He had to get to the air base. He floated underwater for a while then swam to the other side. When he reached there, the guard saluted and let him in. He took the box out of his pouch and showed it to Six and the captain.

Ash Robarts

Ysgol Y Preseli, Crymych

The Walking Blind

I stand here strong and powerful but especially unwanted! I feel like I don't belong here, I need to find where I belong! It's a dark, loud and evil place. No one will help me walk these streets or even give me a helping hand with anything! I know they see me as they brush against me and push me down! I need to go the distance to find where I belong and see if someone cares about me there. I must not give up on my dream of living the life that I want to live, a seeing one!

Hafwen Jenkins (12)
Ysgol Y Preseli, Crymych

YoungWriters
Est.1991

YOUNG WRITERS
INFORMATION

We hope you have enjoyed reading this book – and that you will continue to in the coming years.

If you're a young writer who enjoys reading and creative writing, or the parent of an enthusiastic poet or story writer, do visit our website **www.youngwriters.co.uk**. Here you will find free competitions, workshops and games, as well as recommended reads, a poetry glossary and our blog.

If you would like to order further copies of this book, or any of our other titles, then please give us a call or visit **www.youngwriters.co.uk**.

Young Writers
Remus House
Coltsfoot Drive
Peterborough
PE2 9BF
(01733) 890066
info@youngwriters.co.uk